Dear Parents,

Welcome to the Scholastic Reader series. We have taken over 80 years of experience with teachers, parents, and children and put it into a program that is designed to match your child's interests and skills.

Level 1—Short sentences and stories made up of words kids can sound out using their phonics skills and words that are important to remember.

Level 2—Longer sentences and stories with words kids need to know and new "big" words that they will want to know.

Level 3—From sentences to paragraphs to longer stories, these books have large "chunks" of texts and are made up of a rich vocabulary.

Level 4—First chapter books with more words and fewer pictures.

It is important that children learn to read well enough to succeed in school and beyond. Here are ideas for reading this book with your child:

- Look at the book together. Encourage your child to read the title and make a prediction about the story.
- Read the book together. Encourage your child to sound out words when appropriate. When your child struggles, you can help by providing the word.
- Encourage your child to retell the story. This is a great way to check for comprehension.
- Have your child take the fluency test on the last page to check progress.

Scholastic Readers are designed to support your child's efforts to learn how to read at every age and every stage. Enjoy helping your child learn to read and love to read.

— **Francie Alexander**
Chief Education Officer
Scholastic Education

ISBN 0-439-47101-X

Copyright © 2005 by DC Comics.
Batman and all related characters and elements
are trademarks of and © DC Comics.
All rights reserved. Published by Scholastic Inc.
SCHOLASTIC, CARTWHEEL BOOKS, and associated logos are
trademarks and/or registered trademarks of Scholastic Inc.

Library of Congress Cataloging-in-Publication data is available.

10 9 8 7 6 5 4 3   05 06 07 08 09

Printed in the U.S.A. 23 • First printing, May 2005

BATMAN™

DOUBLE TROUBLE

Written by **Percival Muntz**

Illustrated by **Rick Burchett**

Batman created by Bob Kane

Scholastic Reader — Level 3

Cartwheel
B·O·O·K·S

GCLS/GLASSBORO BRANCH
2 CENTER STREET
GLASSBORO, NJ 08028

SCHOLASTIC INC.
New York Toronto London Auckland Sydney
Mexico City New Delhi Hong Kong Buenos Aires

CHAPTER ONE

HALF-CRAZY

Bruce Wayne was one of the richest men in Gotham City. He lived in Wayne Manor, above a secret cave — the Batcave!

That's because Bruce was also Batman!

Every evening, Batman carefully checked his crime-fighting tools and equipment. Then he would go out on patrol.

In Gotham City, all was quiet. And
then an alarm went off. Two-Face and his
gang were robbing Gotham City's First
National Bank!

Two-Face cut the bank safe into two pieces with a big laser. Then he told Lefty and Righty to go inside and take half of the money.

"Why not take *all* of it, boss?" said Lefty.

"I have my reasons!" said Two-Face. "Now do as I say or you'll get on my bad side!"

Lefty knew better than to argue with Two-Face. Lefty and Righty took half of the money from the bank vault. They carried it outside, put it into Two-Face's getaway car, and drove away.

THEY PUT *HALF* THE MONEY IN *TWO-FACE'S* GETAWAY CAR.

HARVEY DENT...

...TWO-FACE!

Once, Two-Face had been a lawyer named Harvey Dent. He had been Batman's best friend. Together, they had sent many criminals to jail. But then an accident left Harvey with bad scars on half of his face.

Harvey became a criminal and called himself Two-Face. He was obsessed with anything that had two sides, anything that was a pair, and anything that had the number two.

Batman was in the Batcave. All of a sudden, he got a call from Police Commissioner Gordon.

"Batman! Two-Face and his men are robbing the First National Bank! Get over there, quick!"

"I'm on it!" said Batman.

With the flick of a switch, he turned on the Batmobile's booster rockets and took off!

THE BATMOBILE ROARED TO LIFE!

In the getaway car, Two-Face had a smile on his face. He tossed a silver coin in the air.

"Good work, boys," he said to Lefty and Righty.

Just then, the Batmobile came speeding around the corner. Two-Face and his men drove as fast as they could.

"Batman's right behind us!" yelled Righty.

"Unless we stop the Batmobile, we'll never get away!" said Righty.

"Quiet!" said Two-Face. "I have to make a decision."

TWO-FACE HOLDS UP A COIN.

CHAPTER TWO

THE GIVEAWAY GETAWAY

The Batmobile was closing in fast.

"We can throw the money out to distract Batman so we can get away," said Two-Face. "Or we can give ourselves up, because the Batmobile will catch us."

"No!" yelled Righty. "We can't get caught!"

"I'm not going back to jail!" said Lefty.

Whenever Two-Face had a choice to make, he would flip a special coin. One side of the coin was normal. The other side was scratched. If the scratched side came up, Two-Face would choose to do something bad.

"The choice isn't ours—it's up to the coin!"

TWO-FACE'S SPECIAL COIN...

said Two-Face with an evil grin. Two-Face
tossed the coin into the air and caught it in his
palm. It landed with the scratched side faceup.

"Throw the money out the window!"
shouted Two-Face.

"But, boss, we just stole it!" Lefty said.

"Do it!" yelled Two-Face. "Then Batman
will never catch us!"

People stood on the sidewalks of Gotham City. They watched as the Batmobile chased Two-Face's car through the streets. Suddenly, thousands of dollars flew out the windows of Two-Face's speeding car!

People ran out into the street to grab the falling money. Batman had no choice. He slammed on the brakes to avoid hitting the people. By the time Batman got everyone to give back the money, Two-Face was gone!

PEOPLE *RAN OUT* TO GRAB THE *MONEY!*

CHAPTER THREE

THE FIFTY-FIFTY FELON

Later, Commissioner Gordon and Batman stood outside of the First National Bank.

"This just isn't Two-Face's style," said Gordon. "Why wouldn't he rob the Second National Bank? It has the number two in its name."

"Two-Face is up to something," said Batman. "I'm just not sure yet what it is."

The First National Bank robbery was just the beginning. Night after night, Two-Face and his gang committed more crimes all around Gotham City. They cut statues in half with a handheld laser. Then they stole only the left halves.

They also broke into the Gotham City Museum and stole halves of world-famous paintings. Even Batman was confused. These "halfway" crimes made no sense at all!

That night, Batman was flying in his Batplane. He saw the Bat-Signal in the sky. But only half of it was lit up. He landed on the roof of police headquarters.

TWO-FACE AND HIS GANG CUT STATUES IN HALF...

...THEN THEY STOLE ONLY THE LEFT HALVES!

HALF THE BAT-SIGNAL WAS MISSING!

Commissioner Gordon was waiting for him.

"Don't tell me Two-Face took part of the Bat-Signal, too," said Batman.

"That's not the half of it," said Gordon. He showed Batman pictures of the latest crimes. Last night, Two-Face had stolen half of the George Washington statue in front of City Hall.

"Why would Two-Face steal half of a statue of the first president?" said Gordon. "Why not John Adams, the second president?"

"Or even Thomas Jefferson, the president on the two-dollar bill," said Batman.

"Slicing the statue in half makes it

worthless!" said Gordon.

"Maybe," said Batman, "or maybe that's what he wants us to think. Do you still have the other half of the statue?"

"Yes," said Gordon. "It's in our evidence room. Why?"

"I'd like to look at it," said Batman. "I think I may know what Two-Face is up to."

HALF OF A STATUE IS WORTH- LESS!

CHAPTER FOUR

Down in the Batcave, Batman studied the half-statue on his giant Batcomputer.

Alfred walked in carrying a tray with tea and sandwiches.

"Master Bruce," said Alfred, "did you buy that at a half-off sale?"

"Very funny, Alfred," said Batman. "This

statue is actually worth nothing."

"I should think so," said Alfred. "Half of it is missing!"

"Actually," said Batman, "it was worth nothing before it was cut in half. It's a fake!"

"But why would anyone cut a fake statue in half?" asked Alfred.

"If everyone, especially the police, believed the original statue had been destroyed, no one would go looking for it," said Batman. "Robbing the bank and stealing half of the money was a clue, but I didn't see it until now. Two-Face is committing half-crimes. He steals priceless works of art and then replaces them with wrecked copies. That way, he could have the world's greatest art collection and the police would never know!"

"That's very clever!" said Alfred. "And he almost got away with it."

"He still might," said Batman, "unless I let him steal the Wayne Family Ming vase!"

"Master Bruce!" said Alfred. "That vase is one of the most valuable pieces in your collection."

"Don't worry, Alfred," said Batman. "I promise to bring it back . . . in one piece!"

CHAPTER FIVE

DOUBLE OR NOTHING

The next day, the newspaper ran a story that Bruce Wayne's priceless Ming vase was on display at the Gotham City Museum.

That night, Two-Face and his men broke into the museum, stole the vase, replaced it with a half-wrecked fake, and sped away in their car.

ON THE *ROOF* OF THE BUILDING STOOD *BATMAN,* WATCHING FROM THE *SHADOWS.*

TWO COATS PAINT COMPANY

Two-Face's car slowed to a stop at an abandoned factory. The sign on the building read: TWO COATS PAINT COMPANY. The two henchmen went inside.

On the roof of the building stood a dark figure in a cape—Batman! He peered through a skylight. Inside, the large room was split down the middle into two halves. On one side were valuable works of art. On the other side were identical copies. Two-Face set the vase down on one side of the room.

ON ONE SIDE WERE REAL WORKS OF ART...

...ON THE OTHER SIDE WERE FAKES.

"I can't believe Batman hasn't figured it out," said Two-Face, laughing. "He thinks I'm stealing halves. He doesn't know I'm actually making doubles!"

"But, boss," said Righty, "if everyone thinks all these things have been destroyed, how are we gonna sell the originals?"

"It's easy," said Two-Face. "We'll offer them to private collectors. Since they'll know these pieces are stolen, they won't show them to anyone. Then, when they realize we've sold them a fake, they can't tell the police!"

"We're going to sell fakes?" said Lefty.

"Yes!" said Two-Face. "We can sell doubles of these works of art forever! We'll make a fortune! And we'll be surrounded by the world's most valuable pieces of art!"

"No, you won't," said Batman, stepping out of the shadows. "The only thing you'll be surrounded by are prison bars!"

"Batman!" yelled Two-Face. "How did you find us?"

"With the Bat-tracer on Bruce Wayne's vase," said Batman.

"It doesn't matter," said Two-Face angrily. "You're outnumbered by my men, two to one! And you wouldn't dare fight us in here. Look around you. One side of the room is filled with priceless works of art, and the other side has fakes. You don't know which is which!"

"But I do know, Two-Face," said Batman. "My Bat-tracer tells me exactly which side is right...and you're on the wrong side!"

"Lefty, Righty, get him!" shouted Two-Face. Batman leaped at the two henchmen.

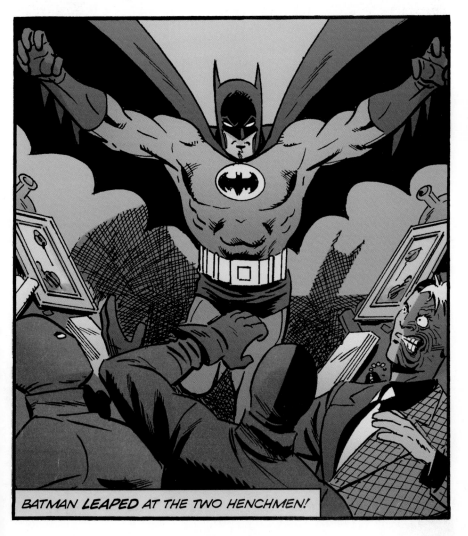

BATMAN *LEAPED* AT THE TWO HENCHMEN!

Batman pushed them into paintings and smashed vases over them. At last, he tied up Lefty and Righty.

LEFTY AND RIGHTY WERE *NO MATCH* FOR BATMAN!

BATMAN *TIED* THEM UP.

CHAPTER SIX

HEADS UP!

TWO-FACE STARTED TO RUN.

BUT HE TRIPPED!

AND THE LASER WENT FLYING!

Meanwhile Two-Face knew he had to get away. He started to run, but then he tripped over a painting. His laser fell out of his pocket and slid across the floor—all the way to Batman!

"Oh, no!" Two-Face shouted. "Do I get my laser back? I might get caught! Or do I escape? I have to make up my mind!" He pulled out his coin and tossed it high in the air.

BATMAN SHOT THE
LASER, CUTTING
THE COIN IN HALF!

"Too late, Two-Face!" said Batman. "I've made up your mind for you!"

And he grabbed Two-Face's laser. He aimed it at the spinning coin. With a *hiss*, the beam sliced the coin in half in midair!

"No!" screamed Two-Face as the two halves hit the ground. One half of the coin landed good side up. The other half of the coin landed bad side up. Two-Face didn't know which decision to make.

TWO-FACE DIDN'T KNOW WHAT TO DO.

BATMAN *SNAPPED* THE CUFFS ON TWO-FACE.

As Two-Face stood there, Batman came up and snapped Batcuffs on him. Then he called Commissioner Gordon on the radio in his Utility Belt.

"This isn't fair," said Two-Face. "My plan should have worked. It wasn't half bad."

"No, Two-Face," said Batman. "Any crime *you* think up is *all* bad!"

Fluency Fun

The words in each list below end in the same sounds.
Read the words in a list.
Read them again.
Read them faster.
Try to read all 15 words in one minute.

actually	collection	booster
carefully	lotion	commissione
definitely	nation	computer
especially	relation	lawyer
suddenly	station	silver

Look for these words in the story.

evening	pieces	special
caught	giant	

Note to Parents:

According to *A Dictionary of Reading and Related Terms*, fluency is "the ability to read smoothly, easily, and readily with freedom from word-recognition problems." Fluency is necessary for good comprehension and enjoyable reading. The activities on this page include a speed drill and a sight-recognition drill. Speed drills build fluency because they help students rapidly recognize common syllables and spelling patterns in words, and they're fun! Sight-recognition drills help students smoothly and accurately recognize words. Practice these activities with your child to help him or her become a fluent reader.

—**Wiley Blevins,**
Reading Specialist